W9-CYH-030

E
GUT

Guthrie, Donna.

Nobiah's well.

$15.00

| DATE | | | |
|------|------|------|------|
|  |  |  |  |
|  |  |  |  |
|  |  |  |  |
|  |  |  |  |
|  |  |  |  |
|  |  |  |  |
|  |  |  |  |
|  |  |  |  |
|  |  |  |  |
|  |  |  |  |
|  |  |  |  |
|  |  |  |  |

BAKER & TAYLOR BOOKS

# NOBIAH'S WELL

## A MODERN AFRICAN FOLKTALE

BY DONNA W. GUTHRIE ✦ ILLUSTRATED BY ROB ROTH

IDEALS CHILDREN'S BOOKS · NASHVILLE, TENNESSEE

CHAMPAIGN PUBLIC LIBRARY
AND INFORMATION CENTER
CHAMPAIGN, ILL. 61820

This book is dedicated to Lifewater International.
                                                    – D. G.

For Debbie and Jason.
                        – R.R.

Text copyright © 1993 by Donna W. Guthrie
Illustrations copyright © 1993 by Rob Roth

All rights reserved. No part of this publication may be reproduced or
transmitted in any form or by any means, electronic or mechanical,
including photocopy, recording, or any information storage and retrieval
system, without permission in writing from the publisher.

Published by Ideals Publishing Corporation
Nashville, Tennessee 37214

Printed and bound in the United States of America.

Library of Congress Cataloging-in-Publication Data is available.

ISBN 0-8249-8622-9 (trade)
ISBN 0-8249-8631-8 (lib. bdg.)

The display type is set in Lithos Bold.
The text type is set in Berkeley.
Color separations were made by Wisconsin Technicolor, Inc.,
New Berlin, Wisconsin.
Printed and bound by Arcata Graphics, Kingsport, Tennessee.

Designed by Joy Chu.

First edition
10  9  8  7  6  5  4  3  2  1

# Long ago

IN A FAR-OFF LAND WHERE IT HAD NOT RAINED FOR

MANY YEARS, THE SUN BAKED THE EARTH TO A

CRUSTY BROWN, AND THE WIND BLEW THE DUST FROM

HERE TO THERE. IN THIS HOT, DRY PLACE LIVED A

YOUNG BOY NAMED NOBIAH.

He lived with his mother and baby sister in a simple hut made of dry grass and mud. Beside their hut grew a small patch of green they called a garden. Nobiah and his mother tended each plant with love and care because the food they grew was all they had to eat.

Each morning, just before daybreak, Nobiah's mother rose and went with the other village women for water.

Because the closest well was a long way off, Nobiah's mother would spend most of her day walking to the well to fill her clay jar with water and bringing it home again. Some water was for drinking, some for cooking, and some for cleaning, but most of the precious water went into the dry earth to make their garden grow.

One morning Nobiah's mother did not rise from her sleeping mat. Instead she called to him, "I am sick today, my son. You must go to the well and bring back a jar of water for us to drink and for the tender, young plants that grow in our garden." Nobiah picked up the clay jar and balanced it carefully on his head. Walking across the dusty

Because the closest well was a long way off, Nobiah's mother would spend most of her day walking to the well to fill her clay jar with water and bringing it home again. Some water was for drinking, some for cooking, and some for cleaning, but most of the precious water went into the dry earth to make their garden grow.

One morning Nobiah's mother did not rise from her sleeping mat. Instead she called to him, "I am sick today, my son. You must go to the well and bring back a jar of water for us to drink and for the tender, young plants that grow in our garden." Nobiah picked up the clay jar and balanced it carefully on his head. Walking across the dusty

land, he followed the village women toward the well, which was many miles away.

When he arrived at the well, the line was long. Nobiah waited patiently for his turn. And when it was time, he dipped his jar into the well and brought out fresh, clean water to take back to his mother.

As Nobiah started home, he could feel the weight of the heavy jar on his head and the fierce African sun shining down on his back. He had not gone far when he met Kalunguyeye, a small hedgehog.

"Nobiah, Nobiah," said Kalunguyeye, "give me water to drink. For I am thirsty, and I need water from the well!"

Nobiah had a tender heart, and he knew too well the parched, dry feeling when there is nothing to drink. Feeling sorry for the hedgehog, Nobiah knelt and dug a hole with his bare hands in the dry, hard ground. He filled the hole with water, and Kalunguyeye drank quickly before it disappeared into the parched earth. When the hedgehog finished, he hurried away without another word.

Nobiah continued on his way, but the jar felt lighter. Further along Nobiah found Fisi, a hyena mother, sitting in the high grass with her cubs.

"Nobiah, Nobiah," said Fisi, "give me water for my young cubs. They are thirsty and need water from the well!" Nobiah looked at the two hyena cubs nestled at their mother's breast. He thought of his baby sister sheltered safely in his mother's arms, and his heart was touched.

Nobiah knelt again and once more dug a hole in the hard, dry ground. He filled the hole with water for Fisi and her cubs. The three hyenas drank quickly before the water disappeared into the dry earth. When they finished, they ran off into the brown grass.

Nobiah picked up the clay jar, which was lighter now, and walked on toward home. Just outside his village he saw a small ant bear, Muhanga, tangled in a trap. Muhanga, who loved the night, was slowly dying in the heat of the late day sun.

Quickly Nobiah freed Muhanga and bathed his head in water. The ant bear's long, dry tongue reached out again and again for something to drink.

Nobiah held the water in his hands for the thirsty Muhanga while the ant bear drank and drank.

When he was finished, Muhanga said, "Thank you, my friend. Your heart is as big and deep as the well that gives this water." And then he hurried away.

When Nobiah returned home, his baby sister ran out to meet him, for she was very thirsty. Nobiah poured a cup of water for his sister and one for his mother.

"Take some for yourself and then throw the rest on the tender young plants in the garden," said Nobiah's mother. "The day was hot, and they are withered and dry."

But when Nobiah raised the jar, barely a drop of water fell. The jar was empty.

"What has happened to all the water?" cried Nobiah's mother.

"I gave some to a hedgehog, a hyena, and an ant bear," said the boy.

"But why?" asked his mother. "Why would you waste precious water on animals?"

"They feel the same thirst as we do," said Nobiah.
"Their tongues are hot and dry like ours from the
sun and the drought."

Nobiah's mother was so angry that she picked up
the empty jar and threw it against the wall of her
hut, where it broke into a hundred little pieces.

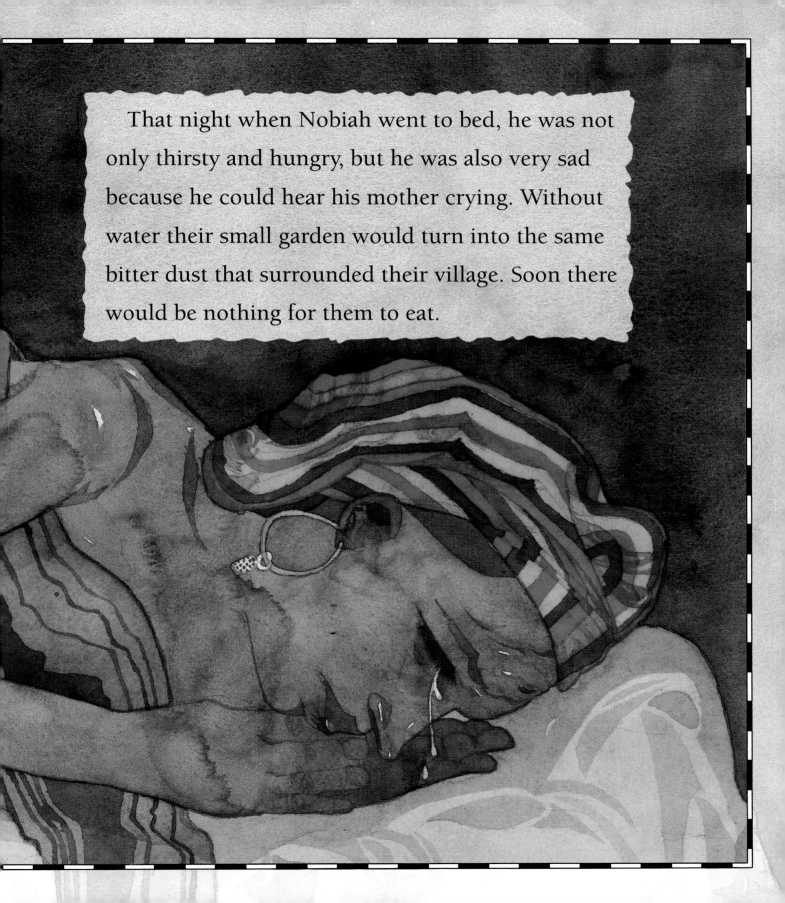

That night when Nobiah went to bed, he was not only thirsty and hungry, but he was also very sad because he could hear his mother crying. Without water their small garden would turn into the same bitter dust that surrounded their village. Soon there would be nothing for them to eat.

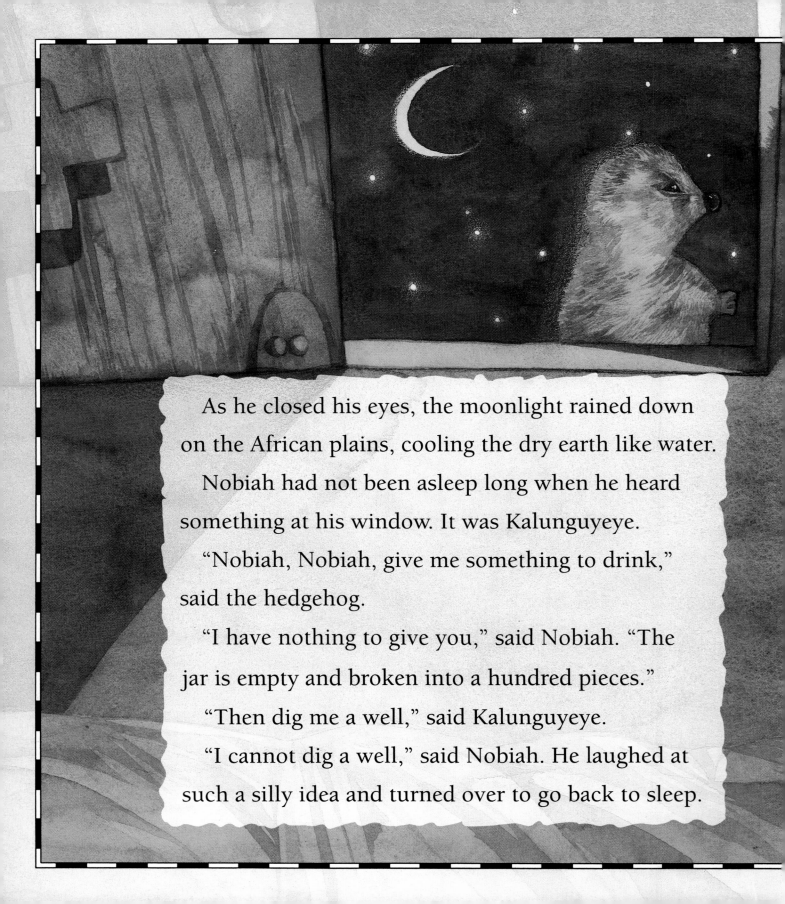

As he closed his eyes, the moonlight rained down on the African plains, cooling the dry earth like water.

Nobiah had not been asleep long when he heard something at his window. It was Kalunguyeye.

"Nobiah, Nobiah, give me something to drink," said the hedgehog.

"I have nothing to give you," said Nobiah. "The jar is empty and broken into a hundred pieces."

"Then dig me a well," said Kalunguyeye.

"I cannot dig a well," said Nobiah. He laughed at such a silly idea and turned over to go back to sleep.

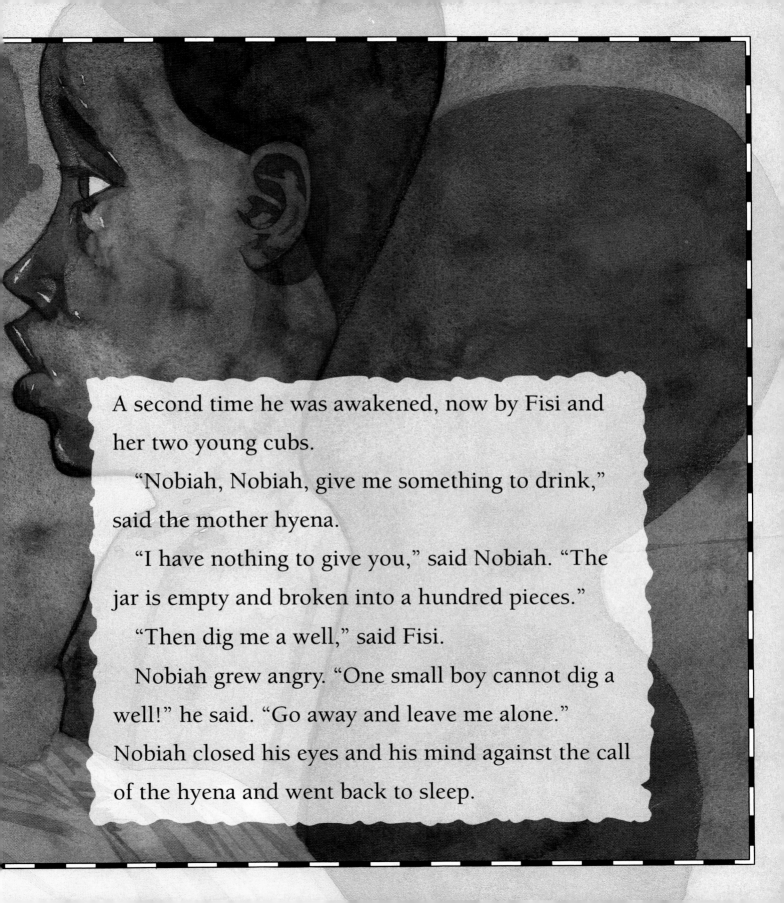

A second time he was awakened, now by Fisi and her two young cubs.

"Nobiah, Nobiah, give me something to drink," said the mother hyena.

"I have nothing to give you," said Nobiah. "The jar is empty and broken into a hundred pieces."

"Then dig me a well," said Fisi.

Nobiah grew angry. "One small boy cannot dig a well!" he said. "Go away and leave me alone." Nobiah closed his eyes and his mind against the call of the hyena and went back to sleep.

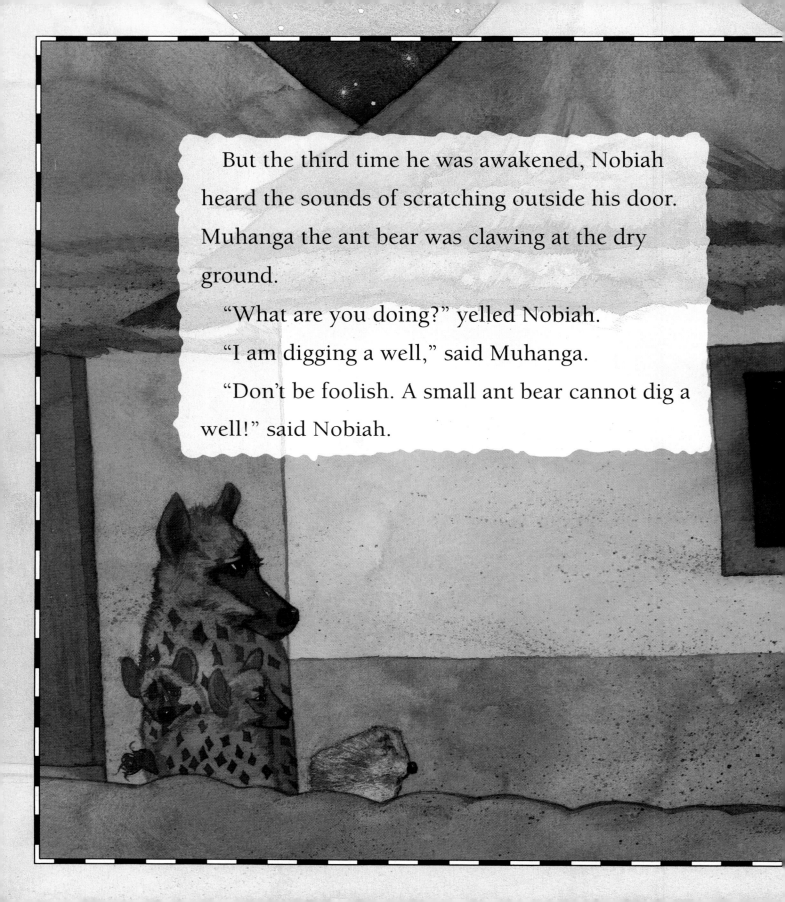

But the third time he was awakened, Nobiah heard the sounds of scratching outside his door. Muhanga the ant bear was clawing at the dry ground.

"What are you doing?" yelled Nobiah.

"I am digging a well," said Muhanga.

"Don't be foolish. A small ant bear cannot dig a well!" said Nobiah.

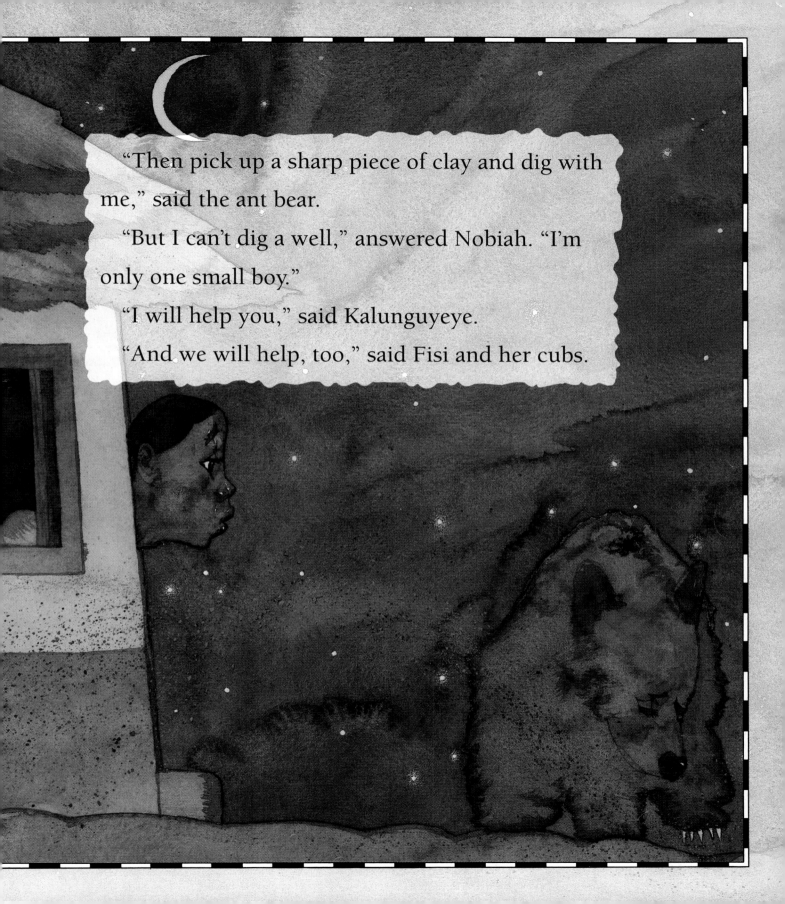

"Then pick up a sharp piece of clay and dig with me," said the ant bear.

"But I can't dig a well," answered Nobiah. "I'm only one small boy."

"I will help you," said Kalunguyeye.

"And we will help, too," said Fisi and her cubs.

With his powerful curved claws, the ant bear dug deep into the ground and in a few seconds vanished from sight. Fisi and her cubs moved the dirt from the opening of the hole while the small hedgehog ran round and round in a circle, making the earth level and flat.

Nobiah picked up a piece of the broken jar and knelt beside the others. He dug, too, sometimes carrying the dirt and sometimes smoothing the dirt, each time asking, "How deep must we dig, Muhanga? How deep must we dig?"

"As deep as your heart," said Muhanga, "and as wide as your thirst."

Finally tired and thirsty, Nobiah fell asleep. But his animal friends worked through the night until the rays of a new day began to outshine the moon.

When Nobiah awoke, he heard the sounds of water trickling deep from within the hole. Beside him there was a beautiful clay pot with strange markings on it.

Nobiah lowered the jar into the hole, which was very deep and very wide, filling it with fresh, pure water. After tasting the water, he called out to his mother and sister and the other villagers, "Come quickly! We have a well of our very own!"

After that the women of Nobiah's village did not have to travel long distances for water. They stayed at home to tend their gardens and care for their children. And the dry desert around Nobiah's village became rich fields of green.

And the clay pot with the strange markings was kept by the well forever to remind all who saw it that when digging a well it must be deep as your heart and as wide as your thirst.